Lucy's Wi

Mary has been writing books for children and teenagers for fifteen years, and has now had more than 50 titles published. She writes funny stories, animal stories, spooky stories and romantic stories, and before she started *Lucy's Farm* she spent some time in Devon to be sure she got all the details right. Mary has two grown-up children and lives just outside London in a small Victorian cottage. She has a cat called Maisie and a collection of china rabbits. She says her favourite hobby is "pottering", as this is when she gets most of her ideas.

Titles in the LUCY's FARM series

1. A Lamb for Lucy
2. Lucy's Donkey Rescue
3. Lucy's Badger Cub
4. A Stormy Night for Lucy
5. Lucy's Wild Pony

Coming soon

6. Lucy's Perfect Piglet

All of the LUCY'S FARM books can be ordered at your local bookshop or are available by post from Book Service by Post (tel: 01624 675137).

LUCY'S FARM

Lucy's Wild Pony

Mary Hooper

Illustrations by Anthony Lewis

MACMILLAN CHILDREN'S BOOKS

First published 2000 by Macmillan Children's Books
a division of Macmillan Publishers Limited
25 Eccleston Place, London SW1W 9NF
Basingstoke and Oxford
www.macmillan.com

Associated companies throughout the world

ISBN 0 330 36798 6

Text copyright © Mary Hooper 2000
Illustrations copyright © Anthony Lewis 2000

The right of Mary Hooper to be identified as the
author of this work has been asserted by her in accordance
with the Copyright, Designs and Patents Act 1988.

1 3 5 7 9 8 6 4 2

A CIP catalogue record for this book is available from
the British Library

Phototypeset by Intype London Ltd
Printed and bound in Great Britain by Mackays of Chatham plc, Kent

Chapter One

"Do you know any ghost stories about this area?" Mr Beale, the Tremaynes' new Bed and Breakfast guest, asked Lucy over his bacon and eggs on Saturday morning.

Lucy smiled at him and shook her head. "Nothing, I'm afraid," she said politely. She took a mouthful of cornflakes. "Nothing at all."

"Mr Beale's writing a book about local myths and legends," Lucy's mum, Julie Tremayne, explained to her daughter. She laughed. "Lucy isn't much interested in

1

ghosts," she said to Mr Beale. "Doesn't believe in them. She's more your outdoors and animals sort of girl."

"Ah, well," said Mr Beale, sounding disappointed.

Lucy's mum brushed her shirt free of the cornflakes which Kerry, Lucy's little sister, had deposited on her. She was a tall, attractive woman with hair as blonde as Lucy's. "And I'm afraid *this* house isn't haunted, if that's what you were hoping."

Their guest laughed. "No. I didn't think it was. I just wondered if there were any local stories you might know about. Anything weird at all."

"Well, let me think," Julie Tremayne pondered. "I did hear once . . ."

As her mum recounted a local tale, Lucy mentally went over the things she had to do before her best friend Bethany Brown arrived and they went up to Rotherfield Moor to work on their school project.

Lucy was going to be busy. She had to collect that morning's eggs from the chicken coop, then she'd promised Donald, her donkey, that she'd give him a good grooming – and she also had to feed two baby calves with some of the fresh creamy milk that had been produced by the herd that morning.

Lucy, her mum and dad and little sister Kerry, lived on Hollybrook Farm in Bransley, a village in the Devonshire countryside. The Tremaynes had a herd of fifty or so black-and-white Friesian cows, a clutch of chickens, a small flock of sheep – including Rosie, a lamb Lucy had bottle-fed since Rosie was an hour old – and Roger and Podger, two cross-bred collies. This was as well as Donald, of course, and a variety of farm cats that slunk about in quiet corners hoping to come across a tasty mouse.

"So you haven't heard any spooky

stories at school?" Lucy's mum asked her now.

Lucy shook her head, her tousled blonde hair swinging from side to side. "The only local things we're doing this term are mushrooms and fungi," she said. "What varieties grow where – in woods or fields or moors – which you can eat, and which are poisonous. Stuff like that. That's why Beth and I are going up on the moor this afternoon – we've got to find as many different kinds as we can."

"That's all very useful," Mr Beale said, peering at Lucy over his wire-rimmed glasses, "but not to me, I'm afraid. I'm looking for stories set in this part of Devonshire in the olden days – and the stranger the story the better I'll like it!"

"I'll see if Beth knows anything," Lucy promised, thinking that Mr Beale seemed quite nice. Unlike some! That was the trouble with doing Bed and Breakfast, she thought – you were never sure what the guests were going to be like. Having people to stay meant the family earned a little extra money, though, and Lucy's mum was specially pleased to have someone staying now, in November, when the regular season for tourists was over.

Mr Beale pushed his plate to one side and stretched back in his chair. "That was a good breakfast," he said. "Just how I like it. Were the eggs and bacon from this farm?"

"Well, the eggs are ours," Lucy said. "The chickens are laying really well at the moment."

"But the bacon's from the shop in the village," her mum finished.

"You've no pigs here, then?"

Lucy's mum shuddered. "If there's one thing I can't stand, it's a pig!"

"Oh, Mum!" Lucy protested. "Pigs are

lovely!" But before she could go on to tell her mum just *why* they were lovely, her dad, who'd just finished milking the cows in the milking parlour across the lane, pushed open the front door. Roger and Podger, who'd come in with him, bounded through the boot lobby – where their baskets were kept – and straight into the kitchen. They ran up to Lucy excitedly, their muddy paws leaving a good deal of farmyard mud over the grey slate floor.

"Out!" Lucy's mum roared, making everyone jump. She glared down at the dogs. "Get out at once!"

As the dogs slunk back into the boot lobby, Julie Tremayne looked at Mr Beale and flushed slightly. "Sorry if I startled you," she said, "but those dogs know they're not allowed in here. They're absolutely covered in mud."

"That's because they like rolling in puddles," Lucy said, helping herself to a piece of toast and her mum's home-made marmalade.

Tim Tremayne removed his muddy boots, came into the kitchen and said a cheery good morning to everyone. He was a large, ginger-haired man who, because he was always outdoors, tended to have a tan and freckles whatever time of the year it was.

"Mr Beale's writing a book about local legends," Lucy's mum said to him.

"Spooks and spectres, weird and wonderful happenings – I write 'em all down. I've had several books published," said Mr Beale.

"You don't know of anything weird around here, do you?" Lucy's mum went on. "I said he should go and have a word with the vicar. I know there's some tale about that huge old yew tree in the churchyard having a coffin inside it."

Lucy's dad went to the sink to wash his hands. "I've never heard of that," he said. "There's the Dancing Maidens up on the moor, though. Twelve girls turned into stone because they danced on a Sunday."

"Yes, I know about those," Mr Beale said.

"They do say that once a year the maidens come to life," Lucy's dad said with a grin. "But if you believe that you'll believe anything!"

As everyone laughed, Lucy's dad turned

to her. "When you've finished your breakfast, love, there's a couple of calves waiting for theirs."

"I'm going right now!" Lucy said, stuffing the last crust into her mouth and taking her plate to the sink. "Have a good day!" she said to Mr Beale. "I hope you find the spooky stories you're looking for."

"Oh, I'm sure I shall!" Mr Beale said, and Lucy thought how jolly he seemed for a man who collected tales of ghosts and ghouls.

Lucy went into the boot lobby to put on her wellington boots and – because it was a chilly morning – a thick old anorak, then went into the farmyard to collect eggs from the chicken coop.

There were no chickens in the coop – they were all out pecking around the yard, so Lucy lifted the little wooden doors and felt amongst the straw to discover how many eggs they'd laid. A while back, Freckles the chicken had gone broody and hatched ten chicks. Now they'd grown up and started laying eggs themselves, the Tremayne family had rather more eggs than they needed. Lucy's mum sometimes took them to sell at the village hall market.

"Seven eggs," Lucy muttered to herself. "Well done, chuckies!"

She collected the pale brown eggs – some of them still warm – in a bowl and passed them through the kitchen window to her mum. Then she went over to feed the calves, who had their own small living quarters, fenced off from the bigger cows, in the steel barn opposite the farmhouse. The herd lived in the barn all winter, only going to the field down the lane in the spring, when the weather was warmer.

The two calves Lucy's dad had mentioned were nearly a week old and already drinking milk quite well from a bucket. They just needed a bit of encouragement to take solid food. Neither of them had the slightest idea what to do with a mouthful of hay! Lucy thought it was a bit like Kerry: when they'd first tried to get her to eat some cereal, she'd just sat there with a spoonful of it in her mouth, not seeming to realize she had to chew and swallow it.

The calves were twins – two girls, so the Tremaynes would be keeping them to join the herd later. Each had the usual black-and-white Friesian markings and dark, long-lashed eyes. They reminded Lucy of Daisy, a little calf she'd helped into the world all by herself. Daisy was now in the proper herd.

"Eat up! Lovely hay!" Lucy said to the calves encouragingly, pushing tiny bundles of hay into their mouths. Little by little the sweet-smelling hay went down, with plenty of milk afterwards.

It took a good half-hour to persuade the calves to eat all they should, and Lucy was glad it was a Saturday – she knew her dad would never have been able to spend as much time fussing over them as she had. She couldn't wait until she was grown-up and could leave school and work on the farm full-time. Better still, have a farm of her own!

From the barn, Lucy went down the lane to the paddock – a small field close to the farmhouse – to collect Donald, her donkey. Donald lived outside most of the time; in fact, he seemed to quite like the cold weather. What he didn't like was when it was hot and he was bothered by flies, so during the summer months Lucy usually brought him into the little hay barn in the farmyard.

"There's my lovely boy!" Lucy put her arm around Donald and he gave a short welcoming bray. Luckily the sheep were all grazing up the far end of the field, so Lucy was able to get out before Rosie saw her and rushed up for attention. Lucy led Donald back to the farmyard, got out her brushes and spent a good hour on him, making his coat gleam. Donald stood still, enjoying the attention, giving small grunts of pleasure every so often. He was a very different donkey indeed from the sad creature she'd rescued from the beach the previous summer.

When Lucy had finished she tethered him up loosely in the hay barn – she knew her dad might need him to help carry some feed to the sheep later – and then kicked her boots off and climbed the ladder up to her bedroom.

The top floor of the little hay barn might have been rather a strange place to have a bedroom, but Lucy loved it there. At first, when her parents had asked her to move out of the farmhouse to make more room for the Bed and Breakfast guests, she'd been a bit put out. Once she'd settled in, though, she hadn't minded a bit. Her room was low-beamed, quaint and cosy. *And* she was near the animals.

She got out her homework book to remind herself what they had to do on the moor for the project. She and Beth both went to the local village school, and Mrs Fern, their teacher, had asked the class to go mushroom and fungi gathering. They

14

were to collect as many different types as they could, and then name, label and describe them ready for a display in the hall the following week. Some of the others were looking in the woods or fields, but Lucy and Beth had chosen to go to Rotherfield Moor to find theirs. Lucy was really looking forward to the trip. Not because of the mushroom hunt, though – because of all the wild ponies that lived there.

Engrossed in her book, time passed quickly. It was about midday when Lucy heard voices from downstairs in the yard. Then came a call. "Lucy! Are you up there?"

It was Beth. Lucy grabbed her jacket and a box she'd made to put the mushrooms in. "Just coming!" she called back.

"Hi, Lucy!" came another voice, and Lucy's heart sank. *Courtney*! Don't say *she* was coming with them too!

15

Chapter Two

Lucy didn't much like Courtney. There were two reasons: one was that Courtney used to live in London and never stopped going on about how fantastic it was there compared to Bransley. The second was that Lucy – who'd been best friends with Beth for ages and ages – felt that Courtney was trying to take Beth away from her. And now Courtney had turned up uninvited!

Lucy went down the ladder to speak to the two of them, trying very hard to keep a smile on her face. Courtney, she noticed straight away, had six sparkly clips in her hair. She was also wearing a sleeveless silver puffa jacket, pale blue trousers and white trainers. Not very suitable, Lucy thought, for a freezing cold day on the moors.

"Courtney rang me and asked if she could come with us," Beth said. "That's all right, isn't it?"

"Course," Lucy fibbed, trying to keep the smile going. "What happened to Lindsey, then?"

Lindsey had been Courtney's partner – Mrs Fern had insisted that everyone went out looking for fungi in twos or threes.

"I didn't want to go with her," Courtney said in a whiny voice. "I wanted to be with Beth."

Lucy would have liked to say something sarcastic, but thought she'd better not. "I expect it'll be really cold up there," was all she said, looking at Courtney's clothes.

"Oh, I'll be all right," said Courtney. She pulled a face at the old anorak Lucy was carrying. "Anyway, I'd rather be cold than look frumpy."

Lucy really *was* about to say something this time, but Beth stepped in, waving a book in the air. "I've got this really good book from the school library," she said quickly. "It's got practically every mushroom in Britain in it. We can look up everything we find."

Sighing to herself, Lucy realized that if she didn't want a full-scale row she was just going to have to put up with Courtney. "And I've made this box to put them in," she said, showing them a cardboard shoe box with a string handle.

"Any calves to feed before we go?" Beth asked hopefully. Her family lived in a house in the village but didn't have any pets – not even a cat – so Beth liked to share Lucy's animals whenever she could.

"I've just fed the two newest ones," Lucy said. "We can do them again when we come back, if you like." She shrugged her arms into her jacket. "Shall we get going?"

Beth asked if they could go and have a quick look at Rosie before they went, and the three girls walked up towards the paddock. The sheep were still at the far end, nibbling at the short grass, but before they reached the gate Lucy called, "Rosie! Come on then!"

They heard an answering bleat, and then Rosie left the small flock and literally galloped up to the gate of the paddock, baa-aaing like mad at the sight of Lucy.

They all laughed. "I love the way she comes to you when you call!" Beth said.

"That's because she thinks I'm her mum," Lucy said. "Hand-reared lambs always do that."

Beth bent over the gate to ruffle Rosie's fleece. "She's so lovely and fluffy. I wish I could take her home."

"You can borrow her if you like," Lucy said. "Put her in your back garden – sheep are better than lawnmowers!"

Courtney was looking at Rosie a bit distastefully. "Shall we go, then?" she said. "Have we got to walk far?"

"It's about a mile," Lucy said. As

Courtney's face fell, she added, "Mum said she'd give us a lift up there, though. We can spend a couple of hours finding stuff and then walk home."

"All that way back!" Courtney wailed, but Lucy pretended not to hear her.

Back in the farmyard, Lucy's dad lectured them about not going too far onto the moor. "I know you're sensible girls," he said, "but it's all too easy to walk further than you intend. Just keep a central landmark in view and don't stray too far off the main path."

The three girls nodded.

"If the weather turns, start back at once – whether you've got all the stuff you need or not. And stay away from Bracken Bog."

"What's that?" Courtney asked.

"It's a thick, muddy swamp, and it's dangerous because it's hidden by plants and undergrowth. You can find yourself completely stuck in mud before you know it," Lucy's dad said.

"We'll watch out," Lucy said. "We'll be careful."

Mr Beale had just come into the yard. "Keep your eyes open for anything mysterious, won't you, girls?" he said. He looked at Lucy's dad and scratched his head. "Bracken Bog, did you say? I read a story about that somewhere. Can't quite remember what I read, though."

"In the middle of the bog there's a pool which is said to be bottomless," Lucy's dad said. "No one's ever been able to work out quite how deep it actually is."

"Oh yes? Jolly interesting," said Mr Beale, and he adjusted his glasses, took out a notebook from his inside pocket and jotted something down.

Lucy's mum came out holding Kerry's hand and with a basket of eggs over her arm. "I'll drop you three up on the moor

and then I'm going down to the market with these eggs," she said. "Even if I don't sell them I can exchange them for some nice local cheese."

"D'you girls want to take the dogs with you?" Lucy's dad asked.

Lucy glanced at Roger and Podger, who were sitting by the back door looking hopeful. She shook her head. "I'd rather not, Dad," she said. "They bounce around too much! Mushrooms are really delicate –

the dogs are bound to jump all over them and break them."

Roger and Podger seemed to know they were being rejected and looked at Lucy sadly, heads on one side.

"See how they're looking at you," Lucy's dad teased her. "They know you don't want them!"

"Besides," Lucy went on, "I'd like to try and get close to the wild ponies and they won't come to us if the dogs are around."

"I shouldn't think they'd come near you anyway," her dad said. "They're too nervous."

"But we've more of a chance without the dogs," Lucy said.

Lucy's mum fitted Kerry into the toddler seat in the Land Rover, then stowed her eggs safely on the parcel shelf. Lucy, Beth and Courtney climbed in the back.

"Hold on tightly!" Lucy's mum said. "It'll be a bit bumpy in the back."

Lucy's dad opened the five-bar gate for them. "Take care!" he shouted. "And don't bring any of those ponies home with you!"

Chapter Three

"There they are. There are the ponies!" Lucy said to Beth and Courtney excitedly. It was lovely to be up on the moor again. And *brilliant* to see the ponies.

"It's all so . . . so vast!" she said, staring about her and marvelling at the wildness and openness of it all – taking in the purple heather and the bright yellow of the prickly gorse bushes, and the way the soft grey moorland seemed to blend, further off, into mist and sky.

Lucy's mum had dropped them in the lane just by the cattle grid – a section of

26

iron bars set into the road which stopped the ponies from coming down into the village. From here they'd walked up a stony pathway and come to a ragged hedge of briars which led onto the moor.

"I'd forgotten how wild it is!" Lucy said to the others, and she ran into the wind with her arms outstretched, pretending to herself that she was a kestrel. "It's all blustery and bleak and blowy!"

Courtney shivered loudly, hugging her arms round herself. "It's blowy all right," she complained. "It's *freezing.*"

"You should have had that jacket my mum offered you," Lucy said.

Courtney pulled a face of horror. "It was *brown*!"

Lucy didn't say anything, just gritted her teeth. She had a feeling that her teeth were going to be gritted quite a lot that afternoon . . .

"Shall we go right up to the ponies?"

Beth asked. "I've got a couple of flapjacks in my pocket. Shall we feed them?"

"We can try," Lucy said, "but they'll be quite shy. I expect they'll run away." She stared at the ponies. There were about twenty of them in the group nearby – and another group a little further off. Most of them were dark brown, although there were about three lighter, chestnut-coloured ones, a couple of grubby greys and a black-and-white piebald. They all looked rather thin, scruffy and uncared-for.

"How did they get here?" Courtney asked, staring at them. "Who do they belong to?"

Lucy shrugged. "No one, really. This is common land – no one actually owns it – but a couple of times a year the hill-farmers round up the ponies and take them to market to sell. It's called the Drift."

The three girls slowly made their way

towards the ponies. Lucy was making encouraging noises, and Beth's hand was stretched out, holding a flapjack. As the girls grew closer, though, the ponies shied nervously, edging away. Suddenly the piebald pony took fright, neighed and galloped off, and the others followed. When they were some distance away, the ponies settled down a bit and carried on eating grass, looking up at the girls every so often to make sure they weren't coming any closer.

"They're not used to people," Lucy said. "Hardly anyone comes up here in the winter."

Courtney turned her back. "Oh, never mind them. Let's get on with it," she said. "The sooner we finish the sooner we can go home."

Lucy gritted her teeth again. Why had Courtney come in the first place? she wondered. Probably just to make sure that she and Beth didn't spend any time on their own together.

"Shall we start by looking under that gorse over there?" said Beth, pointing to some yellow bushes nearby. "I'll get the book out."

But just as Lucy was about to start for the bushes, her attention was caught by the sight of a pure white pony which had appeared among the others.

"Oh, look!" she said. "What a beautiful white pony! Where did *he* come from?"

The two girls turned. "Where?" Beth asked.

"Over there . . . near that big chestnut one!" Lucy said, trying to see round the other ponies which had got in the way. But the white one seemed to have disappeared.

Lucy frowned, puzzled. "Oh! It's gone."

"Are you sure you saw it in the first place?" Courtney asked.

"Course I am," Lucy said scornfully. She knew what she'd seen all right – a very pretty, pure white pony. "Why should I make it up?"

Courtney shrugged. Beth, who'd been gingerly lifting the branches of the prickly gorse bush to look underneath, shook her head. "No! There's no mushrooms here." She pointed out a fallen tree in the distance. "Mrs Fern said you often get fungi on dead trees," she said. "Shall we try over there?"

As they started walking towards the tree, Courtney began talking about a new band and how she was going to get tickets to hear them when they came to play nearby. "D'you want my mum to get a ticket for you too, Beth?" she said. "They're *brilliant*."

Beth nodded. "How about you, Lucy?" she asked.

"I'm not sure," Lucy said, feeling un-comfortable. She pointed at something on the trunk of the tree. "That's a fungus, isn't it?"

Beth nodded and peered further down the tree. "And I think that's a different one there." She got out her book. "Oh yes!" she exclaimed. "This one's a honey fungus." Muttering, she thumbed through the pages. "And I think this one is called

velvet shank. Look at the picture – d'you think it's the same?"

Lucy looked and nodded. "That's two we've got already!" She waved her cardboard box. "I'll break a couple off and put them in here to keep them safe."

Beth looked at the book again. "Neither of them are poisonous. It says here they can be used to flavour stews or casseroles."

"I don't think we'll bother!" Lucy said.

Half an hour later they still only had two specimens in their box, and Courtney was saying she was bored.

"The two we've got will do, won't they?" she said in a whining tone. "It's getting really cold now. My feet are *freezing*."

Lucy wanted to say that it was her own fault for not wearing thick socks and wellies, but she didn't. "Mrs Fern said we were to try and get at least five varieties," she said.

"Well, there are no more here, are there? We're walking round and round the same spots. Why can't we go further onto the moor? I bet we'd find some really good ones."

Lucy shook her head, looking up. The clouds overhead had thickened and the sky had a strange yellowish tinge to it. "We mustn't go too far," she said. "We've got to stay fairly near the path, just in case the weather turns nasty."

Beth pointed. "There are some big old stones right over there. Perhaps they've got some fungus growing on them."

Lucy nodded. "Let's have a look. I think we can still see the path from there."

"Oh – are these the Dancing Maidens?" Beth asked as they approached the tall, grey stones, which were ranged round in a loose circle.

"I think so," Lucy said. "I haven't been up here for ages. I've only seen them once before."

"What d'you mean – Dancing Maidens?" Courtney asked, curling her lip scornfully.

"Oh, it's just an old legend," Beth said. "Hundreds of years ago, a group of girls were supposed to have come up here, and there was a picnic and music and dancing. Apparently it was a Sunday, though, and they shouldn't have been here. They were turned into stones as punishment."

Courtney shrieked with laughter. "What rubbish! No one believes that, do they?"

Lucy shrugged. "Not really," she said. "It's just one of those stories – like fairies and things." She looked around for the ponies. The herd was some distance off now, nibbling the short grass, occasionally giving a whinny or neigh which carried across the moor on the wind. Lucy would have loved to have gone closer and made a fuss of them, but she knew they'd only canter off if she approached.

Suddenly, the white pony appeared again in the middle of the others. Lucy stared at him for some moments. It might just have been her imagination, but he seemed to be staring straight back. She was just about to tell Beth about him though when he disappeared into what seemed to be a patch of mist. Strange, Lucy thought, because it wasn't really misty at all. More bleak and sharp and frosty. She pulled up her anorak collar, shivering a little. She had a yellow woolly hat in her pocket and if the weather got much colder she was going to put it on. Her dad had joked that she looked like a boiled egg in the hat, and it certainly wasn't an item that Courtney would wear, but she didn't care about that. Let Courtney say what she liked!

They reached the Dancing Maidens. Each long stone was of solid grey granite, heavy and immovable. They looked as if they'd been standing there for hundreds of years.

"They don't look much like *maidens*," Courtney said.

"No. And they haven't got any fungi on them, either," Beth said, disappointed.

Courtney gave an exaggerated sigh. "Look, there's another old tree right over there. Let's see if there's any on *that*."

"We'd better not," Lucy said. "It's too far away from the path. It's difficult to tell distances on the moor but I think it's quite a way off."

"So?" Courtney said. "Who's worried?"

"Lucy's dad said not to go too far," Beth said nervously.

"Oh, don't be such a wimp!" Courtney said, flouncing off towards the tree.

Lucy and Beth exchanged worried glances. Lucy took a deep breath. "We'd better go with her," she said. "We shouldn't be separated."

"Oh dear," Beth said nervously.

They set off after Courtney, who was striding along with her head in the air, humming loudly.

Beth gave a sideways glance at Lucy. "Sorry about bringing her," she whispered. "She asked if she could come and I didn't know what to say."

"That's OK," Lucy said. She smiled at her friend, and then suddenly spotted a small, frail mushroom in a clump of grass. "Look! There's one!"

They bent over it and Beth got out her book. "I think," she said, "it's called a fairy-ring champignon. Are there any others?"

They looked around in the soft grass. "I don't think so," Lucy said.

"It says here that they often grow in fairy rings."

Lucy shook her head. "That's the only one."

"Still – one's all we need. Let's put it in the box."

By the time they'd done that and set off again, Courtney was a fair distance away from them, but still hadn't reached the tree. Lucy and Beth started after her, hurrying now, and walked for several minutes without speaking. Breathing in, the air was icy. Lucy was beginning to feel the cold even through her thick anorak.

Suddenly, Lucy stopped and looked hard at the ground beneath her feet. There were clumps of bright green grass, and the occasional wet patch. If she and Beth hadn't been wearing boots their feet would have been soaked.

"The ground is getting boggy!" she shouted at Courtney, who was about twenty metres ahead of them. "Come back!"

"Don't be such a bossy boots!" Courtney shouted back at her. "You can't keep telling me what to do."

An instant later, though, she gave a sudden cry. "My feet are wet. It's really boggy!" Then came a scream. "I'm stuck in mud and I can't get out. I'm going deeper. *Help me*!"

Chapter Four

Beth clutched at Lucy's arm. "What's happened to her?" she said. "Why is she stuck?"

Lucy gave a gasp. "I think . . . I think she must be right on the edge of Bracken Bog."

There was another scream from Courtney. "Don't just stand there! Help me!"

"Remember what my dad said – you can't see where the bracken and marsh plants end and the bog begins," said Lucy, her voice ragged and anxious. "That's why it's so dangerous. You're in it before you know you are, and then the mud sort of sucks you down."

There was another scream. "Get me out!"

"Don't move!" Lucy shouted to her. "Don't move, whatever you do. You'll just sink further in."

There was a burst of sobs from Courtney. She was up to her knees in thick mud and struggling to keep her balance.

"Oh, Lucy! What're we going to *do*?" Beth asked urgently.

Lucy thought hard. They were too far from home to run back – Courtney might have sunk to a dangerous level in the mud before help arrived. "We'd better try and get her out ourselves," she said, thinking aloud.

"How can we do that? We daren't get too close to her in case *we* go in!" Beth said, beginning to cry herself.

Lucy glanced across the moor. The sky was heavy with billowing cloud and it seemed to be getting darker, although it was only two o'clock. Far off, near a clump of gorse bushes, stood the white pony. He was staring towards them and was as still as a statue apart from his tail, which gently stirred in the wind. Lucy knew this wasn't the right time to mention him to Beth, though – and besides, it seemed that she was the only one who was able to see him. "If we could find a branch or a plank of wood or something, we might be able to use that to help pull her out," she said.

They both looked at the tree which Courtney had been making for. "I could probably break a branch off that," Lucy said, "but I'm not sure how safe the ground is around it. I don't want to end up in Bracken Bog myself."

"There were some old bits of wood near the Dancing Maidens," Beth said.

"So there were!" There used to be a wooden noticeboard near the Maidens which gave details of the old legend, but it had fallen down long ago. Lucy remembered seeing some wood there, though. "I'll run back!" she said. She looked round. They'd come much further than she'd realized. "I think I can just see the tops of the stones from here."

45

"What shall *I* do?" Beth said in a trembly voice.

"Nothing. Don't move – I think we're already on the outskirts of the bog. Just shout encouraging things to Courtney," Lucy said. "Tell her what we're going to do. I'll be as quick as I can."

She gave Beth the cardboard box which contained the mushrooms, then stepped slowly and carefully until she was sure she was away from any marshy patches. Only then did she turn and begin running back as fast as she could. As she ran, she looked over towards the dark hills. Heavy, dull clouds were gathering and there was a hint of snow in the air. On the horizon a group of brown ponies could be seen nibbling the grass, but the white one had come closer and was still staring in her direction. It was, Lucy thought fleetingly, as if he was keeping his eye on them. Watching and waiting. But that was being silly, of course . . .

The pieces of wood were half-covered by matted grass and heather. Lucy pulled out the longest bit, getting a splinter in her hand in the process, and began to drag it back towards where Beth waited.

When she got closer she could hear Courtney wailing, "Get me out! What's happening? Hurry *up*!"

Beth was looking terribly anxious. "D'you think it'll work?" she said. "Can you get close enough to pull her out?"

"I'm not sure," Lucy said. "It's difficult to tell from here which bit of ground is boggy, and which is firm." She pointed to just beyond where Courtney was. "I can see a couple of rocks so the ground must be OK over there. If I can walk towards them in a big semi-circle I think I can avoid the bog."

"Be careful!" Beth said. She hopped from one foot to the other. "What shall I do? Shall I come with you?"

"Better not." Lucy tried to smile. "If I get stuck as well you'll be the only one left. You'll have to run for help."

"Oh, don't!" Beth said, horrified. She, too, looked up at the heavy sky. "I don't like it out here now. I wish we hadn't come!"

"It would have been all right if Courtney hadn't been so stupid," Lucy muttered.

Slowly, steadily, she made her way through the marshy patches and edged closer to Courtney, making for the two or three big rocks she'd noticed. Before she put her foot anywhere she prodded the ground ahead with the piece of wood, just to make sure it was firm.

"Oh, do hurry up!" Courtney wailed. "My feet are *freezing*."

Lucy didn't reply – she was concentrating too hard on what she was doing. Reaching the group of rocks, she placed her left foot in a niche between them to balance herself. She then shoved the length of wood out towards Courtney.

"See if you can hold onto this!" she called.

"I can't reach it!" Courtney sounded panicky.

"Try harder," said Lucy. "If you can grab one end of it, I'll be able to pull you out."

Courtney stretched and made an attempt to reach the end of the piece of wood, but failed. "You'll have to get a longer bit!" she cried.

"There isn't one," Lucy said, and she leaned forward as far as she dared, holding the wood tightly with both hands. "Just try and move yourself towards it a little."

Courtney tried to drag her leg out of the cloying mud, which was up to her knees. But she couldn't do it. Unbalanced, she fell forward. "Ow! Oh, help!" There was a squelching sound as she tore free from the mud.

"That's all right," Lucy called. "You've got a bit of leeway now. Reach for the wood again."

"But I'll get soaked!" Courtney flailed forward, almost fell flat in the mud – but reached the piece of wood!

"Fantastic!" Beth cried. "Hold on tightly, Courtney!"

As Courtney grabbed the end of the wood with both hands, Lucy began to pull hard. By using every ounce of strength she possessed, and with Courtney lying flat, squirming in the mud to help herself along, somehow Lucy dragged her forwards. Within moments, Courtney was on firmer ground, staggering to her feet beside Lucy. As the strain on the wood eased, though, Lucy slipped back, twisting her ankle as she did so. She gasped with the sudden pain.

"I'm all wet! I'm freezing!" Courtney cried, her teeth chattering. "I'm freezing and I'm covered in mud."

Beth waved to them, jumping up and down with cold and excitement. "You're out!" she called. "Come on, let's go home!"

Lucy rubbed her left foot, which was twisted awkwardly and really hurt. *Courtney*! Honestly! It wasn't that Lucy expected her to say thank you, but still . . .

"I've hurt my foot," Lucy told the other two. "I think I'll have to wriggle it out of my wellie." She bit her lip. It was very painful to move, but slowly, gingerly, she eased her foot out of her boot.

"What's the matter?" Beth called.
"It's my foot." Lucy pulled her boot free

and gave another sudden gasp of pain. "Ow! It really hurts."

"Try and stand on it," Courtney said.

Lucy put her injured foot down on the ground and tried to put some weight on it. "Ow! *Ouch*!" This time, it hurt her so much that it brought tears to her eyes. She sat down heavily on the damp grass. "I can't walk on it. Really I can't!"

Beth was gingerly making her way towards her friends. "Are you sure?" she asked. "Not even if we help you?"

Lucy shook her head, trying not to cry. She was worried in case she'd broken it. "It really, really hurts. I don't even want to move it."

"What're you going to do, then?"

Lucy shook her head. "I can't do anything." She brushed away a tear. "You'll have to go for help. I'll get my boot back on somehow, and then wait here for you."

"But we can't just leave you!" Beth said, sounding scared.

Lucy pushed her hair out of her eyes and fought hard not to cry. "You'll have to," she said. "There's no choice. I'll be all right," she added uncertainly.

But would she be?

Chapter Five

"But we can't just leave you on your own," Beth said. "I'll stay with you while Courtney goes for help."

Courtney pulled a horror-struck face. "I can't go all by myself! I'd never find my way back to the road."

It had just started to snow – tiny crystals floating to the ground – but none of the three girls mentioned it. Lucy adjusted her position on the cold, damp earth, trying to make herself more comfortable, tucking her knees up to her chest and hugging her arms tightly around herself. "Courtney's

55

right," she said to Beth. "She won't be able to find her way back on her own, so you two had better stay together." Her voice wobbled as she added, "I'll be perfectly OK."

"But how will we find you again?"

"Easy." Lucy shivered. *Would it be?* "When you go back now you'll have to remember the landmarks. Go to the Dancing Maidens first, then you can find the path from there. Follow the path down to the cattle grid and then back to the farm."

"Aren't there any houses on the way? Or a phone box?" Beth asked.

Lucy shook her head. "Nothing. Just go straight back to Hollybrook and tell my dad."

Beth sighed worriedly. "I still don't know. Are you sure you'll be all right on your own?"

"All I'm sure of is that I can't walk,"

Lucy said. She pulled her woolly hat out of her pocket and put it on, glad of its instant warmth over her ears. "You'll *have* to go, Beth. It's about a mile once you reach the road so it'll only take you half an hour or so. If you hurry."

Beth gave another sigh. "OK, then," she said at last. "If you really mean it." She insisted on leaving Lucy her stripy wool scarf, saying that it would at least be a bit of extra warmth.

"Don't forget – Maidens first and then back to the path," Lucy instructed her.

Beth listened intently and nodded, while Courtney huddled her arms around herself, complaining all the time about how cold she was. With many waves and backward glances, the two of them set off. Lucy watched them until, with one last wave of Beth's gloved hand, they disappeared out of sight and into the snow.

And then . . . Lucy was completely

alone. She glanced across the moor; she couldn't see any of the ponies – not even the white one. Where did they go when the weather was bad? She glanced upwards – all she could see was a flurry of white, soft, feathery flakes falling from a dull leaden sky. It must be one of the freak snow-storms they occasionally had on the moors. Lucy had always been thrilled at the sight of snow – just as long as the animals were safe, of course – but she certainly wasn't now. Suppose she got frostbite and all her toes fell off? And she couldn't help remembering the fairy tale – the Little Match Girl, was it? – who'd frozen to death and been found the next day in a drift of snow. Suppose silly Courtney persuaded Beth to go the wrong way? Suppose they were ages finding their way back to get help? Suppose by the time they returned the snow had covered her up so no one could find her?

She pictured Beth and Courtney trudging across the moor, Courtney's designer clothes wet and covered in mud. Lucy thought they'd be able to get back to the Maidens all right – she just hoped they'd be able to find the path after that. The snow was coming down more heavily now and snow concealed landmarks, covered things up, made them look different. Suppose they got lost on the way back?

Feeling horribly sorry for herself, Lucy put her head on her knees and began to cry. She might never see her family and her animals again!

But then, suddenly, there was a nudge from beside her and a soft whinny. Lucy looked up, startled. *It was the white pony*. But she'd looked everywhere and hadn't seen him nearby . . .

Standing close to her and coated with snowflakes, he was the most beautiful sight Lucy had ever seen – his coat shimmering with a frosty brilliance and his eyes dark and lustrous. Lucy put out her hand and the pony gently nuzzled it with his nose, his breath forming soft white puffs in the air.

"You've come over to see me!" she said, marvelling.

She stroked the pony's muzzle. He seemed a creature apart from the other ponies – sleeker, calmer, with none of their nervous timidity. Better groomed too. His coat was smooth and his mane silky, as if he'd been cared for.

"How did you know I was feeling miserable?" Lucy said wonderingly. "You came at just the right time."

The pony whinnied, nodding his head.

"You're not shy at all. You came to cheer me up, didn't you?"

The pony huffed warm breath at her, stretching his neck down so that Lucy could reach his ears and scratch round them.

"You're a lovely boy!" she said softly.

Lucy took a deep breath, feeling much steadier, and dried her eyes on her sleeve. She smacked the palms of her gloves together to dislodge the snow, then squished her fingers together to keep them warm. She began to sing under her breath – anything she could think of, just for something to do. The pony moved a few steps away and stood quietly watching her.

After a while, feeling more cheerful, Lucy bent to pull her woolly hat further onto her head. When she looked up again, the pony had disappeared.

She gave a startled gasp. "Where – how did you go so quickly?" she muttered, looking all round her. "And where have you gone?" There was no sign of him now, just the soft snow falling, slowly coating the gorse bushes and the moorland and the bare trees. Lucy looked at the ground. The snow had already covered the pony's hoofprints, so there was no trace of him ever having being there.

Lucy shook her head, mystified. She felt better now, though, and confident that her dad would turn up soon. She started singing again, and when she'd sung every song she could think of, sung them all over again.

Fifteen minutes passed and the sky grew darker still. A gust of wind blew a flurry of snow into the air and Lucy gave a little cry as it stung her face. If the wind got up really strongly it might blow all the snow against her . . . she could be buried in it!

Lucy glanced across the moor – there was no sign of the pony, but she could see a small hillock a short way off. There seemed to be a slight dip in front of it and Lucy decided she ought to get herself over there. At least it would offer her a little protection. Hopefully she would be able to skirt around Bracken Bog.

She tucked damp strands of hair into her hat, slowly stretched out her right leg and rubbed it. Then she tried to stretch the left one and gave a shout of pain. She'd hoped that resting it might have helped, but it was just as painful as before, feeling swollen and tight inside the wellington boot, which she'd struggled to put back on. Lucy, realising she'd never be able to walk there, knew she'd have to try and crawl to the hillock.

Slowly, painfully, dragging her left foot behind her, Lucy began to make her way towards it. But she'd only gone a short distance when she suddenly found herself wrist-deep in icy water, soaking her gloves and wetting the ends of her sleeves. She must have lost her bearings. Bracken Bog was right there under the greenery and light covering of snow. She just hadn't been able to see it.

Lucy gave a whimper of fright. Another few inches and she could have been caught in the mud. And then what would have happened to her?

She began to move back, slowly . . . slowly . . . inch by inch. But it was snowing harder and she began to get confused, not knowing exactly where she'd come from. She started crying. She was lost on the moor, in Bracken Bog, in the middle of a snowstorm. No one would find her. No one would save her . . .

Chapter Six

A soft whinny came from beside her. It was the white pony again.

Lucy burst into tears. "I don't know what to do," she said, half to herself and half to the pony. "I'm stuck here! I'm going to get in deeper and then I'll drown!"

The pony bent his head towards her, nudging under her arm.

"I can't make a fuss of you now," Lucy said. She stayed stock-still for a moment and tried to think. She mustn't do anything in a rush, she must sort things out in her head first. *Which way should she go?* If she could just work out where she'd come from, she could simply go backwards.

The pony nudged her again and gave a soft whinny. Lucy ignored him. All she could think about was the fact that her jeans were soaked and she was wrist-deep in water that was so bitterly cold it was making her hands ache. She had to *think*. But again the pony nudged her, pushing his muzzle hard into her side and almost moving her along.

Lucy looked up at him in surprise. "You . . . you're trying to push me, aren't you?"

There was a soft neigh in reply.

The realization suddenly hit her. "I think you're trying to help me get out of here!"

Lucy tried to stop crying, and steady herself. It really and truly did seem as if this pony wanted to help her out. If she could just get her arms round his neck, maybe he'd take her to safety – away from Bracken Bog.

But could ponies really help people? Were they capable of sensing when a human was in danger?

Lucy didn't know. What she did know was that this might be the best – the only – chance she had.

She stretched up her arm and grabbed the pony's mane. He whinnied, then moved to one side with Lucy, lifting her away from the danger zone. Half stumbling, clinging to him and putting all her weight on her right foot, Lucy allowed herself to be led away from Bracken Bog.

When they were a few metres off and on firmer ground, the pony stopped and Lucy released her hold on him. Standing on one foot, she stripped off her soaking wet gloves and dropped them onto the snow, then pulled her hands into her anorak sleeves to try and warm them. "Thanks. Oh, thank you!" she said, hugging the pony's neck. "I don't know how you managed it but I think you've saved me!"

She looked around her, trying to see through the swirling snowflakes that swept against her face and clung to her eyelashes. She could still see the small hillock she'd been making for. Breathlessly, she nudged the pony around so that he was facing in that direction. "I want to go *there*," she whispered. Leaning on the pony and hopping painfully alongside him, she moved towards the mound, skirting the bog.

The wind was whipping up the snow into a swirl all around her, but there was a small patch of green showing in the shelter of the hillock, out of the wind. Thankfully, Lucy lowered herself onto it. The pony let her get settled and then, much to Lucy's astonishment, lay down beside her, forming a windbreak that sheltered her from the weather.

"You *know* I'm in danger, don't you?" Lucy said. "You've saved me from going deeper into the bog and now you're keeping the worst of the weather off me." Lucy knew, of course, that horses and ponies rarely lay down, even going to sleep on their feet. Maybe, she thought to herself, ponies were like dolphins – able to sense when a human being was in distress.

She tucked each of her hands into its opposite sleeve and, shivering, tried to rub her wrists to warm herself up. It seemed such a long time since Beth and Courtney had left. Had they reached home yet? Had her dad already set out to find her?

She bowed her wet head onto the pony's back, still hardly able to believe what had happened. This pony had actually rescued her. He had saved her from the pool, and then helped to shelter her from the snowstorm. She couldn't wait to tell them at school on Monday! She wouldn't have any mushrooms to show – unless Beth still had them – but she'd have a fantastic story to tell instead.

Lucy huddled herself into as small a ball as she could and, feeling better now that she had the comfort and warmth of the pony's body beside her, closed her eyes. She'd pretend she was at home, sitting in front of the Aga in the kitchen, eating buttered toast. It wouldn't be long now, surely, before she was actually there. At home. Safe . . .

Beside her, the pony gave a snort and a whinny and Lucy woke up with a start. Dreaming of home, she'd actually gone off to sleep for an instant. She put out a hand and patted the pony to say thank you. She knew she mustn't go to sleep. She mustn't be like the Little Match Girl.

"What would I have done without you?" she said to him. "I'd have been frightened to death up here on my own." She began to sing again to keep herself going, rocking backwards and forwards.

She peered out over the pony's back. The moor was now a blurry haze of white with no trees or landmarks visible. How on earth were they going to find her? And when?

"If you were a black or brown pony it might be better," Lucy said to him softly, running her fingers under his mane for warmth. "As it is, you and I merge into the landscape. A snow girl and a snow horse." She began singing louder, partly because the sound of her own voice was comforting, and partly because she thought it might help her dad to find her.

Suddenly, the pony began to get up. Lucy looked up at him, horrified. "Don't go!" She tried to cling onto his mane and keep him from moving. "Oh, don't go!" she said. "Stay with me! I can't manage without you."

But the pony continued backing away into the snow, bowing his head slightly as if in farewell.

"Don't go!" Lucy shouted after him. "I want you to stay here!" Bewildered, miserably trying to see through the swirling snow, she felt as if she'd just lost her best and only friend. "Come back!"

But there was no trace of the pony. As white as the snow that fell around him, he'd completely disappeared.

Chapter Seven

Faintly, Lucy heard the roar of a car's engine, then came a squeal of brakes and the slamming of doors.

That was the Land Rover. Lucy was sure of it! "Over here!" she shouted. "I'm here!"

A moment after that she heard voices. "Lucy! Where are you? Lucy!" There was a piercing blast on a whistle.

Thrilled, Lucy knelt up. It was her dad! He'd found her! She waved her arms madly. "I'm here, Dad! This way!"

The tall shape of her father came

75

through the snow. And behind him came Mr Beale in her dad's waterproof hat and jacket, his glasses all covered in snowflakes.

Lucy forgot her coldness and fear – she even forgot the pony in her excitement at seeing her dad. "Hurray! You've found me!"

Her dad picked Lucy up in his arms and hugged her. "Thank goodness we got to you so quickly!"

"It's seemed like ages to me," Lucy said.

"Beth showed us the way, and I brought the Land Rover up as far as I could," her dad said. "Thank goodness you weren't too far away."

Mr Beale was standing beside her dad, smiling broadly. "It's snowing back at the farm, but nowhere near as bad as this," he said. He patted Lucy on the back, and then he produced a blanket which he draped around her shoulders.

"Mr Beale insisted on coming out with me to find you," Lucy's dad said, grinning. "I reckon he's going to want to write it up as an interesting local story."

Mr Beale laughed.

Lucy's dad adjusted his hold on her, putting her over his shoulder in a fireman's lift. "Ow! Careful of my ankle," Lucy said, and then added excitedly, "Did Beth and Courtney get back all right? How did you find me? Did you see a white pony?"

"One question at a time," her dad said. "In fact, no questions at all for the moment. Let's just get you home."

He carried her back to the Dancing Maidens, where the Land Rover was. All the time Lucy was looking around for the white pony. He seemed to have disappeared into thin air.

But thank you, white pony, she thought to herself. Wherever you are.

*

"I had a funny feeling about today," Lucy's mum said some fifteen minutes later, handing Lucy a mug of hot chocolate and a home-made biscuit. "When I was dropping you off earlier I just had the weirdest feeling that something bad was going to happen."

Lucy, still rolled into the blanket bundle, had been put into the Land Rover where Beth was waiting, and driven straight back to Hollybrook Farm. As they'd come into the yard Lucy's mum had run out holding Kerry, her face pale and anxious. "I was just about to phone the police!" she said. "Oh, thank goodness you're all right!" And she, too, had hugged Lucy tightly, causing Kerry, squashed in between, to squeal in protest.

Lucy's wellington boot had been cut off and her mum said that though she didn't *think* the ankle was broken, just badly sprained, in a moment they were going to pop Lucy down to the local surgery so it could be checked out. Lucy had changed her wet clothes and was having a warm-up by the Aga while everyone stood around, going over what had happened. Kerry, knowing something important was going on, was silent for once, standing by Lucy's chair and staring at her big sister.

"But nothing really bad *did* happen," Lucy said now. She glanced out of the window into the farmyard, warm, relaxed, happy. Already it seemed like a bad dream! "The weather's not nearly as bad here. Up on the moor it's like one of those scenes in a snow globe!"

"Like Greenland!" Beth put in.

"You're telling me!" said Lucy's dad, rubbing his hair vigorously with a towel. "Lucy was like a human snowball when we got to her."

Lucy's mum sighed and she gave Lucy another hug. "If I'd known the weather would turn so bad up there I'd have come to get you back. You're certainly never going up there on your own again! No matter how many school projects you get given."

"Oh!" Beth clapped her hand to her mouth. "I've left the mushrooms up there!"

Lucy grinned. "Never mind." She looked at her dad. "So because it had started to snow here, you were just setting off to collect us when Beth and Courtney got back?"

"That's right," he said. "Your mum took Courtney home in the old truck, and Beth came with us to get us as near as possible to where you were."

"Which she did most efficiently," Mr Beale said. He was sitting at the kitchen table and making notes on his pad. "Even then, it all got rather tricky. Everything looks the same in the snow, and your dad and I weren't sure of our direction until you shouted to us."

"It was a good job you didn't fall asleep up there," her dad said with feeling. "That's what happens when you get very cold. Everything shuts down."

"I nearly did," Lucy said slowly. "The white pony woke me up." She hadn't been able to say anything about the pony until then because everyone had been so excited and talking at once.

"What d'you mean? What white pony?" her mum said. "You mean a grey?"

Lucy shook her head. "It was pure milky white. And it didn't look like a moor pony, either. It seemed better cared for than that."

"You said you saw a white pony earlier," Beth said to her. "But Courtney and I didn't see it."

Lucy hesitated, shaking her head. "I still don't quite understand about it," she said after a moment.

"What did the pony do, then?" her dad asked.

Mr Beale gave a sudden shout. "White pony! I've just thought of something!" And he disappeared out of the room.

"Tell us about the pony," said her mum.

Lucy decided she'd have to tell them everything – even if her mum never let her out of her sight again. "Well, it's just that the white pony turned out to be a bit of a star." She shot a look at her mum. "He sort of rescued me from Bracken Bog, you see."

Lucy's mum gave a gasp and put her hand to her mouth. "Don't tell me you went in there!"

"Well, yes, I accidentally went a bit too near the water without realizing it, but he practically picked me up and took me to a safe spot. And then – *then* – he stayed with me – lay down beside me and sheltered me from the worst of the wind and snow."

"No!" her mum said, amazed. "Oh, Lucy."

Lucy's dad was scratching his head. "A wild pony did that?"

Lucy nodded. "He stayed with me all the time, keeping me warm and keeping me awake – until just before the Land Rover arrived."

"But that's incredible!" her mum said.

Tim Tremayne shook his head, bewildered. "I've never heard of a pony doing anything like that. Especially a moor pony."

Kerry suddenly grabbed one of her mum's home-made biscuits from the table and thrust it at Lucy. "Eat!" she commanded.

Lucy giggled. "I'm all right," she said. "Really I am. I'm *brilliant* now I'm home!"

Mr Beale came back into the kitchen carrying a cardboard file full of papers. "I've got it!" he said excitedly. "I've found what I was looking for."

"What's that?" Lucy's dad asked.

"Listen to this! I thought I'd heard of a white pony before! This is a pamphlet about the local moorlands which was published nearly sixty years ago." He beamed round at them and then adjusted his glasses and began to read.

"*The Mysterious White Pony.*

Although ponies of all hues are

85

rounded up in the annual Drift, no pure white ponies have ever been brought down from Rotherfield Moor. The following tale, therefore, may be of interest to those of us who believe in the supernatural.

In 1805 Rosamund, the young daughter of the Squire, rode her white pony up to Rotherfield Moor. Although warned of the danger, she strayed too far and foolishly rode her mount into Bracken Bog. Struggling through thick mud, trying to escape, the pony found itself in deep water. It was able to swim to safety, but Rosamund's long skirts and petticoats held her down and, sad to relate, she drowned.

Since that time there have been two sightings of a white pony seen near Bracken Bog. In 1876 one led two young men to safety in a storm, and in 1910 a *white pony saved a girl from dying in the bog. He has not been seen since by human eye, but legend has it that if anyone is in danger on the moor, the white pony will appear again.*"

There was a collective gasp from everyone in the room. Mr Beale put the pamphlet down. "Now, what do you think of *that*?"

Lucy had been listening to Mr Beale with her mouth open. She thought about what had happened – about the way the pony had stopped her from going further into the pool, and the way he'd lain down beside her and sheltered her and stopped her from sleeping.

"I . . . I just don't know," she said at last.

"Still don't believe in ghosts?" said Mr Beale.

"I think," Lucy said nodding slowly, "that I believe in ghost *ponies*!"

LUCY'S FARM 3
Lucy's Badger Cub

Lucy and her friend Beth enjoy watching the badgers in the woods. They are horrified to find one day that all the badgers have gone – except for one little cub.

But there are more mysteries down in the woods. Someone has been living in the old ruined cottage. Can Lucy discover what is going on – and save her little badger cub?

A Stormy Night for Lucy

Lucy is very fond of Buttercup, a cow which her father has just bought. Lucy can't wait for Buttercup's calf to be born!

But when the calf is due, a terrible storm traps Lucy's parents miles from home. And now Buttercup is in trouble. Scared and alone, Lucy knows that only she can bring the tiny calf safely into the world . . .

Collect all the LUCY'S FARM books!

The prices shown below are correct at the time of going to press. However, Macmillan Publishers reserve the right to show new retail prices on covers which may differ from those previously advertised.

Mary Hooper

A Lamb for Lucy	0 330 36794 3	£2.99
Lucy's Donkey Rescue	0 330 36795 1	£2.99
Lucy's Badger Cub	0 330 36796 X	£2.99
A Stormy Night for Lucy	0 330 36797 8	£2.99
Lucy's Wild Pony	0 330 36798 6	£2.99
Lucy's Perfect Piglet	0 330 36799 4	£2.99

All Macmillan titles can be ordered at your local bookshop or are available by post from:

Books Service by Post
PO Box 29, Douglas, Isle of Man IM99 1BQ

Credit cards accepted. For details:
Telephone: 01624 675137
Fax: 01624 670923
E-mail: bookshop@enterprise.net

Free postage and packing in the UK.
Overseas customers: add £1 per book (paperback)
and £3 per book (hardback)